Andy Pandy's weather house

Story by Maria Bird, illustrated by Matvyn Wright

BROCKHAMPTON PRESS, LEICESTER

AND THE POTATO PRESS, CHICAGO

Published in 1973 in the United States of America by J. Philip O'Hara Inc.
Chicago and in Great Britain by Brockhampton Press Limited, Leicester
Published simultaneously in Canada by Van Nostrand Reinhold Limited, Scarborough, Ontario
This edition Copyright © Andy Pandy Limited 1973
Printed in Great Britain by Purnell and Sons Limited

Andy Pandy has a lot of pretty things.
One is a little wooden house with a green
roof and three windows. A little old man
and a little old woman live inside.
Sometimes the little old man stands at the door
and then Andy knows it is going to rain.

But if the little old woman comes out it is
going to be sunny. That is why she carries
a sunshade. One day the White Kitten
jumped up, and just as he did so out
popped the little old woman. So he
dabbed at her with his paw.

But the little old woman was too quick
for him and she darted back into the
wooden house. So the White Kitten
jumped on the roof where he found a
little knob that moved when he touched
it. So he gave it a very hard BANG.

Now just before he did so, the
little old man had crept out and, not
seeing the naughty kitten, he said,
"It's all right, my dear, you can come
out now." So the little old woman
came out with her sunshade.

She was still there next morning
when Andy Pandy woke up. It looked
rather cloudy and dull in the
garden, but as the little old woman
was out, he was sure it was going
to be a fine day.

He wanted it to be fine because
he had promised Teddy that they
should go for a picnic if it were.
So he said, "Wake up, Teddy. The
old lady is out with her sunshade,
so it's the picnic day."

As soon as Andy and Teddy had had
their breakfast, they packed the picnic
basket and set off. They took Looby Loo
in her pram and the White Kitten
came part of the way, but he soon got
tired and trotted back home.

But just as they were sitting down
to eat their sandwiches and drink
their milk, a big raindrop plopped
down into the picnic basket. Then
came another and another, and soon
it was raining very hard indeed.

"Oh dear," said Andy Pandy,
"we'll have to go home."
"It will stop in a minute," Teddy said.
"We can shelter under a tree." But Andy
said no, they must go. As they plodded
home Teddy added his tears to the rain.

But when they reached home it was so nice
and cosy that he forgot his troubles.
Poor Looby Loo was sopping wet,
and Andy put her on a chair near the
fire to dry before he went upstairs
to change his own clothes.

"Give yourself a good rub with a towel," he called
to Teddy, "and change your bow for a dry one."
But Teddy didn't go at once; he stopped to
play with the White Kitten. Now whether
it was because he had cried so much or
because he didn't dry himself, I don't know—

But the next day he had the most
dreadful cold and had to stay in bed.
Andy Pandy was very kind to him and
brought him jellies and gave him nice warm
milk to drink. "Tell me a story, Andy,"
Teddy said. "I'm tired of being in bed."

"Well," said Andy, "once upon a time
there was a naughty White Kitten who
played with the little wooden house
and banged down the knob at the
top so hard that the little people
inside couldn't move at all.

"That is why the little old woman was out
when she should have been in, and why
we went out in the rain when we should
have stayed in, and why you have a cold."
"How do you know?" Teddy asked, sitting up.
"Because I saw him doing it again," Andy said.

"But," he went on, "I made the knob loose
again, so now the little people can move
about, and as soon as your cold is better
and the little old woman comes out with her
sunshade, we'll go back to the fields and
finish our picnic." And so they did.